3/13/18

TO SEEK A
BETTER WORLD

▼

TO SEEK A BETTER WORLD

THE HAITIAN MINORITY
IN AMERICA

BRENT ASHABRANNER

PHOTOGRAPHS BY

PAUL CONKLIN

COBBLEHILL/DUTTON
NEW YORK

Photograph Credits

Embassy of Haiti, 21; Organization of American States, 13 (by Hugh B. Cave), 16, 18; U.S. Army, 23, 24, 25; U.S. Coast Guard, 10. All other photographs are by Paul Conklin.

Text copyright © 1997 by Brent Ashabranner
Photographs copyright © 1997 by Paul Conklin

Library of Congress Cataloging-in-Publication Data
Ashabranner, Brent K., date
    To seek a better world: the Haitian minority in America / Brent Ashabranner ;
    photographs by Paul Conklin.
        p   cm.
    Includes bibliographical references and index.
    Summary: Text and photographs present the Haitian minority of half a million
    people currently living in the United States.
    ISBN 0-525-65219-1
    1. Haitian-Americans—Juvenile literature. [1. Haitian-Americans.] I. Conklin,
    Paul, ill. II. Title.
    E184.H27A84   1997   973'. 049697294—dc20   96-42967   CIP   AC

Published in the United States by Cobblehill Books,
an affiliate of Dutton Children's Books,
a division of Penguin Books USA Inc.,
375 Hudson Street, New York, New York 10014

Designed by Joy Taylor
Printed in the United States of America   First Edition
10   9   8   7   6   5   4   3   2   1

THIS BOOK IS FOR

MARK FRANKEN

Cobblehill Books about Immigration

by Brent Ashabranner

OUR BECKONING BORDERS
STILL A NATION OF IMMIGRANTS

CONTENTS

To Seek a
Better World

Anelia Richard

1

A LITTLE-KNOWN AMERICAN MINORITY

▼

IN JULY, 1994, Anelia Richard left Haiti with her three children. They left with thirty-one other Haitians, mostly men, crowded into an ancient fishing boat with a faulty motor. Their destination was anywhere on the south coast of Florida. For the voyage the boat carried three drums of water, three bags of rice, and one bag of beans. Anelia brought with her only a small bag filled with her clothes and the children's. The bag contained all they had in the world. Anelia had sold everything else she owned to buy their space on the boat. No money was left, not even a Haitian centime.

Anelia was not escaping political turmoil and violence as so many Haitians were trying to do. Her reason for going to the United States was purely economic. She had no particular work skill, and she could not earn enough money in Haiti to feed and clothe her children and herself; she knew she would not be able to send them to school. She did not know what would happen in America, but whatever happened could not be worse that what would happen in Haiti.

On the second day in the Windward Passage between Cuba and Haiti, the boat's engine failed. The boat owner was unable to repair it, and there were no backup sails. For thirteen days the boat and its passengers drifted helplessly on the ocean currents. By the eleventh day the food sacks were empty.

IN THE SUMMER of 1994 hundreds of boats left Haiti with thousands of persons hoping to reach Florida. The U.S. Coast Guard intercepted most of the boats, and during a two-month period interned over twenty thousand Haitians at the U.S. Naval Base in Guantánamo, Cuba. After a hearing by the U.S. Immigration and Naturalization Service (INS), most of those interned would be returned to Haiti.

But the boat Anelia was on was never spotted by a Coast Guard cutter or a Coast Guard search-and-rescue aircraft. Then one night lights of the Florida coastline appeared on the horizon, and in the dark hours after midnight the boat beached near the city of Pompano Beach. No one on the boat knew where they were or what to do, but most scattered into the darkness. Anelia, however, did not run. She gathered her children around her and waited on the beach. Just after sunrise immigration agents found the wet and hungry family and took them to Camp Krome, a federal detention center in Miami where illegal immigrants are held until their cases are decided by the INS.

The United States government defines a refugee as a person who has fled his country "because of persecution on account of race, religion, or political opinion." If a person enters the United States without proper immigration papers and is found by the INS to be a true refugee, he or she usually will be permitted to remain as a legal resident (or in some cases will be given temporary asylum).

Anelia and her children today. After several weeks in Camp Krome, Anelia was able to get a friend in Miami to sponsor her for residence. An immigration judge allowed Anelia and her children to stay. They were given start-up help by a Catholic resettlement program; they receive food stamps, and Anelia earns some money doing domestic work. Her ambition is to learn English, study hairdressing, and work in a beauty shop.

UNLIKE Anelia Richard, Lucknew Lucien was a true refugee from Haiti. He was a supporter of exiled President Jean-Bertrand Aristide and for that reason was harassed by the corrupt and repressive military regime that ruled Haiti. Lucknew's wife and three children fled to an interior village from their home in the capital city of Port-au-Prince, but Lucknew stayed. In mid-1993, police thugs came for him. They murdered his sister, but Lucknew escaped by crashing through a window. He was able to hide until he could get a place on a boat heading for Florida. With his wife and children still hiding in the village, he sailed one night with sixty other Haitians leaving their country.

On the third day at sea, the boat was intercepted by a U.S. Coast Guard cutter. Everyone on the boat, passengers and crew, was taken aboard the cutter for internment at the Guantánamo Naval Base. The empty Haitian boat was burned and sunk as a menace to navigation.

Interviews with INS officials at Guantánamo clearly established that Lucknew was a true refugee in that he had fled from Haiti because of political persecution. He was released from Guantánamo and taken to Miami where he was given settling-in assistance to which legal refugees are entitled by law. The assistance, by both federal and state governments, gives help with housing and provides food stamps for a period of several months. Catholic Charities helped Lucknew look for work. His wife and children in Haiti were allowed to join him in Miami.

Paul and I talked to Lucknew one cool January evening, sitting on the porch of his small rented house in the Little Haiti section of Miami. A not-quite full moon was already visible, and mosquitoes were beginning to buzz. Lucknew's children ran in and out of the house and looked at us curiously but did not stop. I could see his wife in the living room watching television.

Lucknew told us that he and his family were beginning to feel settled in Miami and that all of the children were going to school. He said

Lucknew Lucien

he had been working as a laborer for a television cable company but had been laid off. He hoped to be called back to work soon.

Toward the end of our conversation, Paul asked Lucknew to name one main difference between life in Haiti and life in Miami. Lucknew thought for a moment and then said, "In Haiti if I saw the police, I ran. In Miami, if there is trouble, I can call the police."

THE NEARBY Caribbean country of Haiti is one of the poorest in the world. Eighty-five percent of Haiti's population of 7.2 million lives below the World Bank's absolute poverty level figure. Unemployment, hunger, and malnutrition are rampant. Haiti's infant mortality rate is the highest in the Western Hemisphere. One child out of every five dies before the age of four. Haiti's food production is declining by 2.5 percent every year.

Haiti's government has had a long and troubled history of instability, repression, and insensitivity to the needs and welfare of most Haitians. Beginning about 1980, to escape the increasingly wretched poverty and political violence, thousands of Haitians, much like Anelia Richard and Lucknew Lucien, began coming to the United States every year. Most were young men with little education or training; but many were women, and sometimes whole families came. Whether they were true refugees or came for economic reasons was a meaningless distinction to most. As one of the new arrivals said, "I am a refugee from hunger."

Also like Anelia and Lucknew, they came without passports or other legal immigration papers and traveled the Windward Passage, in small, often unseaworthy boats. Some boats broke up in stormy seas and all aboard were drowned. But between 1980 and 1993 an estimated 200,000 Haitians reached those shores alive and disappeared into the Florida countryside or the at-least temporary shelter of the Little Haiti section of Miami.

Some were caught, interned, and after INS hearings, deported. Some qualified as refugees and were allowed to remain in the United States. Those Haitians who entered the United States illegally before 1982 were — like illegal aliens from all other countries — permitted to apply for legal residence under an amnesty provision of the Immigration Reform and Control Act of 1986. But large numbers of Haitian boat people have remained in the United States as illegal immigrants, surviving as migrant farm laborers, doing unskilled work in cities, or existing on charity.

TODAY THE knowledge of most Americans about people of Haitian ancestry living in the United States is limited to the boat people of the last fifteen years. Throughout those years, newspaper and magazine stories have described the "invasion" of America by poor, illiterate, malnourished, and diseased Haitians fleeing their impoverished and corrupt country. Nightly television news has shown pictures of ill-clothed, barefoot Haitians walking down the gangplanks of U.S. Coast Guard cutters after their boats had been intercepted at sea. The steady flow of these negative stories and images has made Haitians—in the words of a *Washington Post* writer—"the nation's most unwanted immigrants." They are seen as a desperate people with great needs and little to offer the country to which they have fled.

Given the national concern today about illegal immigration, the negative feeling toward Haitian immigrants is not surprising. What most Americans do not know, however, or do not remember is that in the late 1950s and throughout the 1960s thousands of Haitians came to the United States not as boat people but as legal immigrants. (Until 1965 there was no limit to the number of immigrants from Western Hemisphere nations who could come legally to the United States.)

Most Haitians who came during those years did so to escape the brutal regime of François (Papa Doc) Duvalier, the father of Jean-Claude (Baby Doc) Duvalier. François Duvalier became president of Haiti in 1957 with army backing and ruled as a cruel dictator until his death in 1971. Many of those who sought refuge in the United States were well-to-do businessmen and members of the educated professional class, all of whom had most to fear from the tyrannical terror of the Duvalier era. Most of the Haitian immigrants of that time came to New York City where—in the tradition of countless European, Asian, and Latin American immigrants before them—they settled in, adapted to their new country, and raised their families.

A Coast Guard cutter intercepts a Haitian boat trying to reach the coast of south Florida. During the summer of 1994, 20,000 Haitians fleeing their troubled homeland in small boats were intercepted and taken to the U.S. Naval Base in Guantánamo, Cuba, for detention.

Today the Haitian-American population is about half a million. The great majority live in the New York and Miami metropolitan areas, but smaller numbers have settled and continue to settle in other U.S. cities such as Washington, D.C., Chicago, Houston, and Los Angeles. To quote Deborah Sontag writing in *The New York Times*: "They include not only migrant workers in Homestead, Florida, but wealthy doctors on Long Island, not only taxi drivers in Manhattan but college professors in Washington."

The negative image of Haitian Americans is very much on the minds of those who have grown up in the United States, which is indeed their country. Lesly Prudent, a Haitian-American school principal in Miami, seemed to speak for many Haitian Americans when he said to Paul and me: "Because of the media, which concentrates on the boat people and magnifies the negatives about us, the word Haitian does not have a positive ring in the mind of the general public. We want people to know that we are also the doctor, the lawyer, the principal, not just the man fresh off the boat."

Who then are the people who make up the Haitian-American ethnic minority in the United States today? What do they do? What special problems do they have? What are their hopes? What are their contributions to this country? Those were some of the questions that Paul and I wanted to answer in this book.

We think we found the answers and more. But to better understand today's Haitian Americans, we need first to look briefly at the country of Haiti, at its history, and at what is happening there at this time.

2

DAUGHTER
OF AFRICA

A BACKGROUND

NOTE ON HAITI

THE REPUBLIC OF HAITI occupies the western one-third of Hispaniola, the second largest island in the Caribbean. The Dominican Republic covers the eastern two-thirds of Hispaniola. Other nearby islands are Cuba (the largest Caribbean island), Puerto Rico, and Jamaica. Haiti has an area of 10,714 square miles, almost the same size as the state of Maryland, and is less that six hundred miles from Florida.

A country of mountain chains and fertile valleys, Haiti has 850 miles of coastline dotted with fishing villages. The climate is tropical, though not as hot as some tropics because much of the country is at a relatively high elevation. However, Port-au-Prince, Haiti's capital and major port, is one of the hottest cities in the Caribbean.

Village scene today, southwestern Haiti

THE FIRST inhabitants of Hispaniola were Indians from Central and South America. They settled the island as early as 2000 B.C., bringing with them the techniques of agriculture and pottery making. On Columbus's first voyage to the New World in 1492, his flagship was wrecked on a reef off the northern coast of Hispaniola. Columbus left thirty-nine members of his crew on the island and returned to Spain on another ship. When he came back to Hispaniola a year later, Columbus found that his crew-colonists had been killed. He established a new settlement in the part of the island that is now the Dominican Republic and governed there for two years. Named Santo

Domingo, this was the first permanent European colony in the Americas.

During the 1500s Spain controlled all of Hispaniola; but in the early 1600s France, eager for its own New World colonies, gained a foothold in the western part of the island. Spain resisted, but weakened by war with England and more interested in Mexico and South America, recognized France's ownership of the western third of Hispaniola in 1697.

France named its new colony St. Dominigue, and it quickly became the most prized of all French possessions. Colonists from France established great plantations on St. Dominigue, growing sugarcane, coffee, cocoa, tobacco, and indigo. Sugarcane was the major and most profitable crop; millions of tons of sugar were shipped to France every year. The French planters and their families lived lives of extreme luxury, and St. Dominigue became known to Europeans as "the Eden of the New World."

By the mid-1500s almost all of the Indian inhabitants of Hispaniola had died. Originally numbering more than a million, hundreds of thousands had been worked to death as virtual slaves on plantations of the conquering Spaniards; many thousands of others had died of European diseases to which they had no resistance. As a substitute for Indian labor, the Spanish began to import slaves from Africa.

The French colonists quickly followed the Spanish example. They brought in thousands and then tens of thousands of slaves from Africa. By late in the 1700s there were almost half a million slaves in St. Dominigue. In contrast the number of French colonists was quite small: about thirty thousand, including women and children. A third element in the human makeup of St. Dominigue was a population of approximately twenty-five thousand mulattoes, persons of mixed African and European ancestry. These racially mixed persons had been given their freedom and were in fact called *affranchis* (freemen).

Some had become wealthy landowners and slaveholders themselves. They had not, however, achieved social equality with Europeans; they were discriminated against in many ways and were barred from voting or holding political office. The *affranchis* bitterly resented all forms of discrimination against them.

The system of slavery on St. Dominigue was one of unusual brutality. As more and more slaves were imported, living conditions became increasingly worse. Food was inadequate for the labor required of them, and many slaves were literally worked to death. Iron discipline was maintained by cruel overseers, and any infraction of rules or any display of discontent might be punished by torture or even death.

In part the brutality toward slaves stemmed from a deep fear on the part of French planters that someday the slaves might revolt. In 1791 the colonists' worst nightmare came true. In the northern part of St. Dominigue, thousands of slaves revolted. Fighting with machetes, clubs, tools, their hands, they massacred French planters and their families. They destroyed plantation houses, barns, and machinery. They burned crops and tore up irrigation systems. The white colonists fought back with guns and the back-up of French troops, but the revolt spread to all other parts of St. Dominigue, and the free mulattoes—ever jealous of the French power and wealth—joined the fight against the hated colonists.

The bitter struggle raged for years, at times consuming the entire island of Hispaniola. In 1794 France officially abolished slavery in hopes of ending the rebellion but to no avail. Troops from Spain and England became involved because those countries had hopes of making St. Dominigue their colony. But out of the strife rose a great leader, a former slave named Toussaint L'Ouverture, who, although untrained in war, proved to be a military genius. Through his leadership and that of his chief lieutenants, Jean-Jacques Dessalines and Henri

Haitian dancers in fiesta dress

Christophe, who also had been slaves, victory was finally achieved. All French colonists were killed or driven out. French troops, as well as those of Spain and England, were repelled.

On January 1, 1804, the victorious former slaves proclaimed the independence of St. Dominigue; the new country was given the name Haiti, adapted from an Indian word meaning "mountain country." Thus Haiti became the first black republic in the New World and the second independent country (after the United States). The new country had come into existence as a result of the first successful slave revolt in history.

Haiti has been called the daughter of Africa, and the metaphor seems quite appropriate. Except for a small number of colonists, Haiti at the time of independence was populated entirely by people who had been born in Africa or born of African slaves in Haiti. Today, almost two centuries after independence, at least 95 percent of all Haitians still trace their ancestors to Africa. The language, religion, music, dance, food, and folk traditions of Haiti—although influenced by other people and cultures—have their roots in West Africa. Creole, the language of the people, is a mixture of West African and Central African languages and French.

No nation ever began its life with greater liabilities than Haiti. Ten years of savage fighting had left the country in ruins. The economy was shattered. People were exhausted. They had thrown off slavery; but they were without education, and there was no money for schools—and no teachers. There was no knowledge of how to build or run a government. Because Haiti was black and had been born of violent revolution, no other country—not even the United States—would help the struggling young nation.

Distrust between mulattoes and Haitians of unmixed African blood was inevitable and hindered development. Some mulattoes had education and money and used both to gain political power in Haiti. The black masses had the force of numbers, and for 150 years the two sides fought for the leadership of Haiti.

Despite the tremendous problems, the country did have periods of progress. The growing of crops resumed, and coffee became the major export and money-maker. Some schools were opened—the first high school began accepting students in Port-au-Prince in 1818. Many of the big plantations were divided into small plots of land for the peasant population. Attempts were made to create a constitution.

But from the beginning progress was slowed and sometimes completely stalled by political turmoil as regional strong men, rebels, and

Street sellers in front of Iron Gate, Port-au-Prince

ambitious army officers fought for power. Dessalines, the first governor (who called himself emperor), was assassinated. Christophe, the second, committed suicide during a civil war. The third, whose title was president, was overthrown. Between 1843 and 1915 twenty-two different men ruled Haiti under various titles. Most were installed by the army and were dictators. Almost all were assassinated or forced out by revolution.

In 1915 President Woodrow Wilson ordered United States Marines into Haiti. In consecutive years four Haitian presidents had been assassinated or forced out of office, and public order had broken down completely in Port-au-Prince. The country was bankrupt and badly in debt. World War I was raging in Europe, and there were signs that the United States might be drawn into the conflict. President Wilson was concerned that Germany might take advantage of Haiti's anarchy and occupy the country, then use it as a base to attack or harass the United States.

The Marines occupied Port-au-Prince, then extended their control to the entire country, encountering almost no opposition. The U.S. presence in Haiti lasted twenty years, far longer than anyone had expected. Some good things came out of the occupation. Roads and schools were built; health clinics were opened; the government's financial condition improved somewhat; a new constitution was drafted; there were no coups or revolutions.

But there were problems. The U.S. military and civilian authorities brought with them racist attitudes, treating the Haitians as inferiors and favoring light-skinned mulattoes. Haitians were forced to labor on roads and on other public works projects. The humiliation of being occupied by another country led to two attempts at Haitian rebellions. The rebellions were quickly put down by the Marines, but in 1934 President Franklin D. Roosevelt decided the American occupation should end, and all U.S. military forces and civilian administrators were withdrawn. The United States did, however, continue to exert financial control in Haiti until 1947.

WITHIN a few years after the American occupation ended, political chaos returned to Haiti as a series of presidents were overthrown by the army or the police. Some positive things did happen during this period. The University of Haiti was established in 1944. During the term of President Dumarsais Estimé health conditions of the people improved, with many infectious diseases being wiped out. For the most part, however, the government paid scant attention to the problems of Haiti's poor, and their condition remained the same or worsened.

In 1957 François Duvalier became president. A black physician who had been minister of health, he promised to restore power to the people. Duvalier was very popular at first and was given the affectionate nickname "Papa Doc," but he quickly became one of the most repressive dictators in Haitian history. He wanted absolute power, and he created his own private army, called *Tonton Macoutes,* to achieve it. He assassinated or imprisoned anyone who opposed him or anyone he was even suspicious of. Any criticism of his government by the press or other media was forbidden. He rewrote the Haitian constitution and made himself "president for life;" he gave himself power to appoint his successor as president.

Duvalier died in 1971 but not before he named his son, Jean-Claude Duvalier, to succeed as president. "Baby Doc" was only nineteen when he became president. He had no knowledge of how to run a country and no interest in doing so. He was content to live grandly in the presidential palace and entertain his friends. Baby Doc was not as repressive as his father, but he kept the *Tonton Macoutes,* and this paramilitary force continued its evil power.

The young Duvalier infuriated millions of Haitians by marrying a mulatto in an unbelievably lavish wedding that cost an estimated $3 million. Opposition to Baby Doc grew quickly and came from many sources, including the masses of poverty-stricken Haitians and the army. Sixty thousand students marched in the streets of Port-au-Prince in a protest of Duvalier's rules. Although he tried desperately to stay in power, his position became increasingly hopeless. On a night in 1986, Baby Doc Duvalier and his wife boarded an airplane and were flown to France, where they were given asylum.

AS WAS TO BE expected after Duvalier's hasty departure, the

Jean-Bertrand Aristide

Haitian army assumed power, with Lieutenant Gerald Henri Namphy in command. For a time developments seemed promising. A National Council of Government was established, a new constitution was approved, and free elections were scheduled. Though there were delays and attempted political takeovers, an election was held in January, 1991, and Jean-Bertrand Aristide was elected president by a wide margin. A Roman Catholic parish priest, Aristide had devoted his life to the welfare of the poorest Haitians, and his election was received with great joy by the people. In the early months of his administration, Aristide began programs of land reform, reduction of the army and government bureaucracy, and increased educational opportunities.

This bright beginning was not to last. The Haitian military felt threatened by Aristide's programs as did members of the wealthy elite class. On September 30, less than nine months after Aristide's election, his government was overthrown in an army-led revolt. Aristide's great popularity with the people made the army afraid to assassinate him. Instead, the president was abducted in a military coup and exiled to Venezuela. Shortly after that he was permitted to go to the United States.

Led by the United States, the international community condemned the Haitian army's takeover and insisted that Aristide be returned to office. All foreign aid to Haiti was cut off, and a trade embargo was imposed. These actions, however, failed to budge the illegal Haitian military regime. The United States began to build pressure on the Haitian army leader, Lieutenant General Raoul Cedras, and his Chief of Staff Brigadier General Philippe Biamby to relinquish power or face an invasion by U.S. forces.

The ethical or moral rationale for U.S. intervention in Haiti was that democracy should be preserved in the Caribbean country. The practical or "real" reason was to stop the flood of refugees from Haiti trying to reach the United States. The flow of boat people had dropped off sharply after Aristide's election but had resumed again in a steady stream of boats after his abduction and the army takeover.

In the late summer of 1994 it became clear that U.S. forces were going into Haiti within a matter of days. The only question was whether they would face Haitian army forces in an invasion or whether the occupation would be peaceful. Finally, in dramatic, last-minute, face-to-face negotiations, a U.S. team consisting of ex-Presi-

A U.S. soldier talks with curious Haitians at the Port-au-Prince airport.

dent Jimmy Carter, Georgia Senator Sam Nunn, and former Chief-of-Staff Colin Powell persuaded General Raoul Cedras and his staff to resign.

On September 19, at 9:30 in the morning, three thousand American troops from the U.S. Army's 10th Mountain Division descended from Blackhawk helicopters and took control of the airport and ports in Port-au-Prince. The takeover was peaceful and continued to be as thousands of other American soldiers as well as United Nations forces arrived in the following days and weeks.

On October 15, in the midst of wild celebrations in Port-au-Prince, Jean-Bertrand Aristide returned to Haiti to resume his presidency.

There were now fifteen thousand American troops in the country.

American troops encountered no opposition as they occupied Port-au-Prince and other key parts of Haiti.

On the morning of September 19, 1994, three thousand American troops land-ed in Blackhawk helicopters like this one and took control of the airport and ports in Port-au-Prince.

But this time, President Bill Clinton assured the American people, they would not stay for twenty years. They would be out of Haiti in a year-and-a-half. But Haiti was still the poorest nation in the Western Hemisphere. Even with a much-loved president trying to help them, how long would people wait before again trying to take boats to a bet-ter life?

3

LITTLE HAITI

▼

ON MIAMI'S east side, in an area between Thirty-sixth and Eighty-seventh streets, another chapter in American immigration history is being written. This rectangular urban space, approximately fifty by ten blocks, in the past twenty years has acquired the name Little Haiti, and visitors to this section of Miami will quickly see why.

In the residential areas of Little Haiti, small houses painted in lively colors—blue, yellow, green, purple—are intermingled with dull, often run-down apartment buildings built thirty years ago. Those houses and apartments are the homes of more than fifty thousand of the estimated two hundred thousand Haitians who have come to the United States since the late 1970s. Also living here are several thousand Haitian Americans, some U.S. born, who have moved from New York, Boston, Chicago, and other cities to be a part of this new Miami enclave.

Haitian-owned businesses grew slowly in the Little Haiti area at first, but today there are at least three hundred. Most are small, many struggling to survive, but all add to the vibrant life of the community. Traditional Haitian merengue music spills into the streets from record shops and small cafes which feature Haitian foods: goat meat in a spicy red sauce, *griol* (pork cooked with lime), conch in sauce, and everything served with rice and beans. Small businesses selling fruit, groceries, medicinal herbs, and clothes are intermingled with beauty shops, dry cleaners, and a number of Protestant storefront churches. The outside walls of some of the buildings are covered with brightly painted murals featuring religious scenes.

Patterned after a famous market in Port-au-Prince, the Caribbean Market is Little Haiti's business showplace. In a large remodeled building, Haitian small entrepreneurs sell textiles, shell necklaces and bracelets, handmade toys, baskets, straw hats, decorations made from sheet tin, cooking utensils, and dozens of other items. The Caribbean Market also features the paintings of Haitian artists; on most days several artists are at the market working at their easels. Business leaders hope that in time Little Haiti, with the Caribbean Market as its centerpiece, will draw large numbers of Miami residents and visitors to Little Haiti.

Most Little Haiti dwellers are legal immigrants, and their goal still is simply to get by from one day to the next and learn a little more each day about living in a strange new land. There is so much to learn! Speaking their native Creole with friends and neighbors is comforting, but English must be learned in order to look for and hold a job. Enrolling children in a strange school system is a shock for parents as well as children. Miami bus routes must be learned because buses are the link to jobs all over the sprawling, bewildering city. To get a driver's license, to deal with the utility company, to find a doctor or a hospital —all of these things and so many more must be learned.

Even as this learning moves forward at its slow and often painful pace, a new culture is being created. In time it will be dominantly American, but it will be interwoven with Haitian music, dance, food, touches of Creole, strong family ties, faithful church attendance, and memories of family and friends in their former Caribbean homeland. It will be the culture of the Haitian Americans.

Haitians in Miami are, after all, repeating a pattern almost as old as the United States itself. Since our nation's beginnings, immigrant ethnic groups have formed communities in cities—Italians and Puerto Ricans in New York, Chinese in San Francisco, Cubans in Miami, Arabs in Detroit, Mexicans in Los Angeles, Lithuanians in Chicago, to name but a few. These urban enclaves have grown out of a need for support and for reminders of the lost homeland. As they learn to be Americans, immigrants or their children leave these ethnic nests for lives in other parts of the country.

Without exception every immigrant group—the Haitians very much included—has come to America for the same reason: to seek a better life for themselves and their children. For some, a better life has meant living without the threat of religious and political persecution. And without exception, each immigrant group has added to the cultural richness of their adopted homeland.

TOUSSAINT LOUVERTURE Elementary School in the heart of Little Haiti is named for one of Haiti's first great patriots and freedom fighters. A portrait of Toussaint, resplendent in his uniform, hangs in the school waiting room. Underneath the portrait are the words, "Haiti, The First Black Republic in the World." On the opposite waiting room wall is a sign in Creole: *Edikasyone Se Liberasyon* (Education Is Freedom). Despite its name, its location in Little Haiti, and the fact that about 85 percent of its twelve hundred students are Haitian, Toussaint Louverture Elementary is a part of the Florida state school system and teaches the standard state-approved curriculum. (Louverture, without the apostrophe, is an accepted alternate spelling of the Haitian hero's name.)

Lesly Prudent, principal of Toussaint Louverture Elementary School, is a prime example of Haitian Americans who are coming to Miami from other U.S. cities because of Little Haiti and the friendly Florida climate. Prudent came to the United States from Haiti in 1967, when he was eighteen, to join his father who had immigrated to New York in 1956. During all those years his father had sent money back to support his large family in Haiti.

"Luckily for me, my father encouraged me to continue with high school in New York rather than find work," Mr. Prudent told Paul and me and added, "In school the kids called me Frenchy. It's a name that gets hung on a lot of Haitians."

After high school Prudent went to Kingsborough Community College in Brooklyn. He learned tennis there and made the team that won an NCAA championship. Next he transferred to Hunter College in Manhattan where he graduated with a bachelor's degree in physical education. He was number one on the Hunter tennis team, and after graduation became varsity tennis coach and director of the intramural sports program at Hunter.

In 1981 Prudent moved to Miami with his wife and three children. "I was tired of New York weather," he said, "and didn't feel safe there. Another thing, my father had retired and moved to Florida, and I wanted to be closer to him." And the principal added with a smile, "Besides, I fell in love with Miami because it's more like Haiti."

Prudent's first job in Florida was as physical education teacher at Tropical Elementary School in Broward County. After that he taught social studies and other subjects in a middle school and two high schools in the Miami areas. Despite heavy teaching loads, Prudent found the time and energy to earn a master's degree in exceptional

Principal Lesly Prudent visits a class at Toussaint Louverture Elementary School.

education at St. Thomas University in Miami, and he also earned a certificate in educational administration.

Even before he became principal of Toussaint Louverture Elementary School, Prudent was well known in Little Haiti because of two school board-sponsored educational radio programs that he presented each week in Creole: *Radyo-Lekol* (School Radio) and *Ti Kaze Sou Edikasyan* (Small Talk on Education). The programs gave Haitian parents information about American education, helped them understand school rules, and gave advice about how to get older children ready for and into college.

Appointed in 1994, Lesly Prudent is the first Haitian American to be named principal of a school in Florida, and he does not take that distinction lightly. He has the Toussaint facility concentrating on developing the English, reading, and arithmetic skills of the young students; he wants to raise test scores so that they compare favorably with those of other Miami elementary schools.

But Prudent has another goal, and that is to make sure that his students, even as they become Americans, have knowledge of their Haitian roots and take pride in them. Whether they are born in the United States or come from Haiti as young children, the principal says, they become accustomed to American ways much faster than their parents.

Prudent wants his students to have a grasp of Haitian history and culture. He wants them to know about the African-influenced music and dance of Haiti. He wants them to be aware of the country's rich heritage of art. He wants them to understand and prize Haitian traditions of family support and solidarity. Prudent plans to carry out this part of his students' education mainly through after-class clubs and activities and with volunteer help from the community.

Prudent knows from personal experience that young Haitians learning to be Americans will need all of the self-confidence and feel-

Yseult Charles, a lead teacher at Toussaint Louverture Elementary School, with some of her students. Mrs. Charles was born in Haiti and lived there until, as a teenager, she went to Paris and then Chicago with her mother. She spends a good deal of her time counseling parents. "It is a big cultural change for Haitians to come here," she says, "and we Haitian-American teachers can act as a bridge. We can help the newcomers adjust, and we can educate Americans as to what Haitians need." About the children, she says, "It's incredible how quickly they become Americanized. In their first week, they turn up their noses at hot dogs, but a year later they love them. And before long they are saying 'good morning,' instead of 'bon jour.'"

ings of self-worth they can get. "For years people looked at me as though I was just off the boat," he said. "You'll always be reminded that you're a Haitian no matter how much you apply yourself and how much you accomplish."

Principal Prudent shared one tennis memory with us. "I never wore fancy clothes when I played," he said, "so I didn't look like much when I met this fellow on the courts. I had my racket and he said, 'You play tennis?' When I said I did, he pointed to the other side of the court and said, 'Go over there.' A minute later he said, 'I'll serve.' There was no warm-up, none of the courtesy you expect on a tennis court. I'm sure he thought he'd wipe up the court with me, blow me away. I beat him six-love, six-love. You should have seen his face."

The principal permitted himself a smile as he told us the story.

THE CATHOLIC church, Notre Dame d'Haiti, in Little Haiti is a rather ordinary low, white cinder-block building, but the church is surrounded by graceful live oaks, old trees that have survived south Florida's numerous hurricanes. The interior of the church is dark except for early morning sunlight that streams in through lovely stained-glass windows behind the altar. One of the windows depicts Haitian boat people on their way to America.

On Paul's and my first visit to the church, the Wednesday morning mass was attended by perhaps a hundred women, mostly older women, and a sprinkling of men. The mass was said that morning—as it is every morning—by Father Tom Wenski. Father Wenski is a Polish-American priest, but he speaks fluent Haitian Creole and conducts all masses in that language. This was my first opportunity to really listen to Creole; it had a pleasant liquid flow and, to my uninitiated ear, sounded very much like French.

Later we talked with Father Wenski in his office in the Haitian Catholic Center which is attached to the church. Both church and

Father Tom Wenski giving Holy Communion at a morning mass.

center are, in fact, housed in what was formerly a Catholic girls'
school. As we talked, Father Wenski's ancient German shepherd
named Burek lay quietly beside his master's chair. His eyes remained
open, and he seemed to be listening carefully to our conversation.

The priest told us that he graduated from the seminary in 1976,
where his language studies included both Spanish and Creole. He
began work in Miami's Corpus Christi Parish in 1976 and started full-
time work with Haitians in 1979, just as the big influx of immigrants
from Haiti was beginning. The Haitian Catholic Center is Father
Wenski's labor of love and is a beehive of activity from early morning
until late at night. Haitians who work all over the city bring their chil-

(Above) A Sunday morning after-mass crowd at Notre Dame d'Haiti Catholic Church in Little Haiti. Weekday masses are usually lightly attended, but Sunday turnouts are often as high as three thousand.

Ernst Bonny, a New York policeman visiting Little Haiti, whom Paul met outside Notre Dame d'Haiti Catholic Church one Sunday morning. "When I joined the New York police force in the seventies, you could count the number of Haitian patrolmen on one hand," he told Paul. "Now there must be a hundred."

Yolande Thomas. Ms. Thomas is a well-known singer and actress. She has appeared in sixteen plays in New York and Miami and recently made a record of Haitian songs.

dren to the center's day-care facility. Over a thousand adults pass through its classrooms every day and night as they learn English. The center staff offers job counseling, helps with job search, and gives assistance in interpreting often confusing government rules and regulations. Participants pay modest day-care and course fees; the Catholic Church meets other costs of the center. The center also provides space for other organizations that give help to the Haitian community.

Father Wenski runs the Haitian Catholic Center with a small but highly dedicated staff. One of the most dedicated, Yolande Thomas, was born in Port-au-Prince and received a Catholic education there. In 1954, she went to City College of New York and studied accounting. She lived in New York until 1985 when she came to Miami. Working with Haitian priests, she helped open Haitian centers at various Florida locations where refugees were welcomed and helped to find jobs and adjust to living in America.

Father Wenski calls Little Haiti a community in transition. Some businesses are becoming established; others are gone overnight. New people are coming all the time; but others, as they learn English and find jobs elsewhere, are leaving. "An increasing number are moving to north Miami," Father Wenski told us, and he added with satisfaction, "Some are buying houses there."

JAN MAPOU is a man with Little Haiti on his mind and in his heart. He does not live in Little Haiti. His home is in the Miami suburb of Miami Springs, where he lives with his wife and two daughters. He does not work in Little Haiti. His job is at Miami International Airport, where he is administrator of parking. It is a demanding job in which he supervises a staff of one hundred. But Jan Mapou's abiding passion is that the Haitians living in Miami—or anywhere else, for that matter—not lose touch with their cultural roots.

This concern that his countrymen should know and understand

Jan Mapou

their culture and history has been a fundamental part of Mapou's life for over thirty years. In 1965, when he was still living in Haiti and working in a bank in Port-au-Prince, Mapou founded *Sosyete Koukouy*, which means in Creole the "Society of Fireflies."

The purpose of the society was to promote the use of Creole in the schools and in government. The man in the street spoke Creole, but French was then the only official language of Haiti. The society also promoted the idea of teaching young Haitians to appreciate their country's history and culture.

A number of Jan Mapou's friends joined him in *Sosyete Koukouy*, but the society's activities made Papa Doc Duvalier, the Haitian dictator, nervous, and he had Mapou and eleven other society members arrested and thrown into the infamous Fort Dimanche prison. "It was terrible," Mapou remembers. "I was put in a totally dark room. I had no clothes and was given one poor meal a day."

After several months, Mapou and the other members of the society were released from the prison. Mapou knew that he was a marked man in Haiti. With the help of the bank where he had worked, he was able to get a visa to immigrate to the United States and arrived in New York in 1972. In time he became head supervisor of parking at Kennedy International Airport. When some of his friends from Haiti also immigrated to the United States, he started *Sosyete Koukouy* again, this time to help young Haitian Americans learn more about their Haitian heritage.

In New York, Mapou wrote four plays about life in Haiti and directed six others, and they were all produced in the New York Haitian community. "Plays are the best way to reach these people," Mapou said to Paul and me, "the best way to create the reality of Haitian life, especially for young Haitians who may have been born in America and have never been to Haiti." Mapou also wrote articles for a Haitian newspaper in New York and made radio talks.

Nadia (left) and Taina Mapou with their father

In 1984 the company Mapou worked for at Kennedy International Airport won the contract to handle parking at Miami International Airport. Mapou hoped and prayed that he would be selected to set up and supervise the parking there, and he was. With the great influx of Haitians into Miami in the early eighties, Mapou was sure that he and his family should be there.

As soon as his heavy airport responsibilities would permit, Jan Mapou resumed writing on Haitian topics for newspapers and radio and continued his play writing. "I'm the kind of guy who starts working at six A.M. and goes to bed at one A.M.," he said. "As soon as I get home from the airport, I go straight to my computer."

Mapou started *Sosyete Koukouy* in Miami as quickly as he could.

"We need the Society of Fireflies to promote Haitian culture and the use of Creole," he said. "We light up the darkness. We have to find ways to keep our culture alive at a time when young people here in Little Haiti no longer know it. That is our major concern. Many young Haitians speak little Creole or none."

Mapou owns a bookstore, Libreri Mapou, in Little Haiti, which is run by a helper. He sells books about Haiti, both fiction and nonfiction, published in Creole, English, and French. Mapou keeps the store going as a needed cultural resource, not to make money. "I'm not doing very well," he said, "but I have to keep it alive. I have more American customers right now than Haitian. It's a way for them to see who we are, to see that we have feelings just like they do, to learn that we are here to stay, that we're not leaving."

Mapou has written and produced seven plays, all in Creole, since coming to Miami. At least thirty Haitian-American actors participate in his plays, most of them members of *Sosyete Koukouy*. Few make a living at acting, but all have theatrical experience. Mapou's latest play is a musical drama entitled *DPM Kannte*. The letters DPM stand for "Straight for Miami" in Creole, and *Kannte* is the Creole word for a flimsy, unseaworthy boat. Almost the entire action of the play takes place in the boat on the high seas. During the voyage different passengers tell, in words and song, what desperation has driven them to flee Haiti and how they have sold their land, their animals, even their clothes to get money for the trip. The voyage ends tragically in a storm. Everyone aboard is lost except for one—a baby born during the trip. The Coast Guard finds the infant floating on a piece of wood, a tiny fragment of the destroyed boat.

Sosyete Koukouy raised about $15,000 to put on a single performance of the play at Dade County Auditorium. That was a great expense, but there is no doubt in Mapou's mind that it was worth the effort and the money. "There were two thousand people in the audi-

Nadia and Taina Mapou have been dancing since they were eight years old. Here they practice a Haitian plantation dance they will perform in one of their father's productions.

ence," he told us. "Many of them became quite emotional because they, too, had made this same tortured trip. Even the actors were crying."

Mapou is always thinking ahead. "You may be sure," he said, "that the baby who survived will be the subject of a future play."

Jan Mapou's wife is a registered nurse who works at Coral Gables General Hospital. Their twenty-one-year-old daughters, Nadia and Taina, are identical twins. They went to elementary school in Queens, New York, and to high school at Miami Springs Senior High School. They received scholarships to Dade Community College by scoring in the top 10 percent of their high school class. Both Nadia and Taina are actors and both had roles in *DPM Kannte*. They are quietly proud of their Haitian heritage.

It is the kind of pride that people such as Lesly Prudent, Father Wenski, and Jan Mapou are striving to keep alive in the residents of Little Haiti, even as they help them become successful Americans.

4

THE MANY FACES OF HAITIAN AMERICANS

▼

MOST IMMIGRANT nationalities have had to struggle to overcome negative attitudes and sometimes open hostility in order to win acceptance and make their places in America. German, Irish, Italian, Eastern European, and Chinese immigrants of the nineteenth and early twentieth centuries were no exception to this prejudice. Some immigrants such as Arabs from a number of countries are still contending with discrimination and misunderstanding in the United States.

Today thousands of Haitian Americans from many walks of life are helping to create a better understanding and acceptance of Haitian immigrants in America. You will meet some of them in the pages ahead.

Dr. Michel J. Dodard

"I FEEL THAT I have to give something back to the country that raised me. These women need my help. They are members of the working poor with no health insurance. They live completely outside the health-care system."

We were talking with Dr. Michel J. Dodard in a large mobile van parked outside Notre Dame d'Haiti Catholic Church. The van serves as a free clinic for women and children, and Dr. Dodard contributes his time to the clinic every Wednesday afternoon, seeing scores of patients in the course of a month. His patients are the poor people of

Miami's Little Haiti who are trying to find their places in the strange new land they have come to.

Dr. Dodard was born in Haiti in 1950 and went to the University of Haiti Medical School. He was accepted for his residency in Family Medicine at St. Joseph's Medical Center in Yonkers, New York. After completing his residency, Dr. Dodard opened a medical practice in Yonkers and stayed there for nine years. He also received a fellowship in urban medicine from Albert Einstein-Weiler Hospital. In 1988 Dr. Dodard and his family moved to Miami, where he joined the University of Miami faculty. Since 1990 he has been director of the Family Medicine Residency program at the University's School of Medicine.

Dr. Dodard estimates that there are about thirty-five Haitian-American doctors in the Miami area at this time. He has started to enlist the services of some of them for the clinic and foresees the day when they will outgrow the van. He would like a permanent, regularly staffed clinic such as the Cuban-American community has.

When we spoke with admiration for what he has achieved in the United States, Dr. Dodard was modest. "I don't think my accomplishments here are that great," he said. "I really don't. I was, after all, educated when I arrived. But think of the people who arrive in America illiterate and penniless and through the hardest work, sometimes holding two or three jobs at the same time, eventually send their children to Harvard."

DR. LAURINUS (LARRY) PIERRE is a stocky man with a quick smile and a sense of humor. He is also a man with a very serious mission. Born in Leogane, a village south of Port-au-Prince, in 1952, Pierre graduated from high school in Haiti but went to Barrington College in Rhode Island on a scholarship. He returned to Port-au-Prince for medical school and then in 1984 went to the University of Miami for work in internal medicine. In 1988 he received a fellowship

Dr. Laurinus Pierre

for studying the cause and control (epidemiology) of AIDS, which led to a master's degree in public health.

In 1988, Dr. Pierre started the Center for Haitian Studies. It is located in Miami's Little Haiti area, and its purpose is to serve the Haitians of south Florida by educating them in matters of health and health care.

"I started the center with six thousand dollars of my own money," Dr. Pierre told us. "Now we have a million dollar budget with money coming from a number of sources.

"AIDS became my focus," Dr. Pierre said. "The Center for Haitian Studies is the only place in North America where HIV-positive

Haitians can receive the kind of counseling they need. Before this, only non-Haitians, who had no experience with cultural sensitivity, dealt with Haitians. We have a three-hundred-person caseload. We give them direct care, manage their cases, even take meals to their homes if that is necessary."

The center is engaged in various kinds of AIDS research, and in addition has a wide variety of outreach projects. "We give school talks, give technical help to graduate students and health professionals. We distribute AIDS posters and give educational radio broadcasts. We give pediatric care and outpatient specialty care."

The work of the Center for Haitian Studies has a special importance and urgency because of a widespread belief in the United States that Haitians have a higher rate of AIDS infection than other ethnic groups. In fact, in the early years of the AIDS epidemic, the U.S. Center for Disease Control (CDC) designated Haitians as an AIDS risk group. For years, the government barred Haitians from donating blood. The CDC's risk designation has since been rescinded, but public fears and misinformation persist. Dr. Pierre estimates that there may be six hundred cases of AIDS among Haitians out of a Haitian population of 100,000 in the Miami area. If the estimate is correct, that total would be roughly equivalent to the overall AIDS rate for the United States as a whole.

Dr. Pierre is so completely dedicated to his work that we asked him if he ever had any time for his family. "I'm not married," he told us and added with a laugh, "I'll marry when I grow up."

THERE ARE hundreds of Haitian business owners in the Miami area and over two thousand in New York, but few, if any, can match the success of Mireille Gonzales. In 1970 Ms. Gonzales, who was born in Port-au-Prince, was hired by the owner of a camera store in the Miami area. Although she knew nothing about the photographic

Mireille Gonzales

equipment business, she threw herself into the work completely and learned everything about it. In 1978 she and her Cuban-American husband decided to open their own photo-equipment store, for which she would be the buyer and manager.

"I was so scared," Ms. Gonzales said, telling us about the first time she looked around the big empty building they found for their store. "I thought 'How are we ever going to fill this place with merchandise?' But we did, and five years later we opened a second store. Now we have three stores in Miami and one in Miami Beach."

Ms. Gonzales believes she is the only woman in the United States to build and operate a photo-supply business. "My word is more important than my signature," she said, explaining the trust she has developed with both suppliers and customers.

Ms. Gonzales' father still lives in Haiti, and she travels there almost every month to see him. She loves Haiti and told us, "I am always proud to say, 'I am a Haitian.'"

Reverend Bertrand Philippe

IN HOUSTON, the Reverend Bertrand Philippe is pastor of
Mount of Olives Church on the city's west side. One of the many
small Protestant Haitian churches in the United States, Mount of
Olives has only sixty-five members. But although its membership is not
large, those who attend give strong support to the small, well-main-

Mark Laurent is a member of Mount of Olives Church. He arrived in Miami in 1981 during the big build-up of Haitian political and economic refugees. When he could not find work in Miami, Mr. Laurent moved to Houston and has become a custodian in the city school system. A father of five, he is in charge of Sunday school at Mount of Olives Church.

tained church. Mount of Olives also contributes food, books, and money to twelve schools and churches in Haiti.

Mr. Philippe was born in Haiti in 1950 and became a clergyman before coming to the United States in 1978 to live in New Jersey where his brother had settled. Mr. Philippe's first church in the United States was in Brooklyn. He preached and held revival meetings in other cities, including Montreal, before going to Houston.

Although Catholicism was the only official religion in Haiti until 1987, Protestant denominations have had a significant place in the life of Haiti since the mid-1800s, particularly in working with the poorest segments of Haitian society. While only an estimated 15 to 20 percent of the Haitian population is Protestant, about 40 percent of the boat people coming to the United States have been Protestant.

VLADIMIR LESCOUFLAIR is one of a growing number of Haitian-American teachers in Florida. An audiovisual specialist at John F. Kennedy Middle School in North Miami Beach, he is responsible for all communications materials and teaches students how to use television equipment. Every morning they put on a live show for all classrooms, giving school news, sports reports, and announcements of coming events.

Vladimir is not the only teacher in his family. His father, Narces, teaches at Toussaint Louverture Elementary School in Little Haiti; he too is an audiovisual specialist.

Vladimir was born in Haiti, but his family moved to the African country of Zaire when he was three because his father, a teacher, was threatened by the Haitian dictator Papa Doc Duvalier. In 1969, after three years in Zaire, they moved to the United States, settling in Boston. Vladimir went to elementary and high school there. His mother worked in a hospital; and his father, while holding other jobs to help support the family, went to college at night to get his U.S. teaching cre-

Vladimir Lescouflair (right) with student

dentials. After Vladimir finished high school, the family moved to Miami because the climate was more like that of Haiti. Vladimir enrolled in North Miami Beach Community College where he began work in television production.

In addition to his teaching at JFK Middle School, Vladimir produces a weekly TV program called *Sak Pase?* (What's Happening?) for Miami public television. Showing the positive side of Haitian-American life, the program is a mixture of Creole and English and is aimed at a school-age audience. There is a talent segment featuring Haitian-American performers and a history segment which connects Haiti's history to that of the United States.

"If most Haitian-American kids aren't refugees themselves, their parents were, and they feel a little bit out of place," Vladimir says. "We help them build their self-esteem so they can say, 'We are contributing something to this country, too.'"

MARTINE PIERRE-LOUIS and Mugette Guenneguez are good examples of immigrants who leave the traditional urban enclave of a particular ethnic group and seek a life elsewhere in America. Martine and Mugette are sisters who came to New York in 1975 from Port-au-Prince with their parents when they were teenagers. Their father was a lawyer and law professor who had also served as Haitian ambassador to several African countries. Their father decided to leave Haiti because he wanted his family to be in a safer place.

"We lived in a neighborhood in New York where we could hear Haitian music and smell Haitian food and even read our newspapers," Mugette told Paul when he talked to the sisters in Seattle. "We went to school with other Haitian students. There is just a tiny Haitian community here in Seattle. If our family had come directly here from Port-au-Prince, it would have been a major culture shock."

"New York City has neighborhoods that are so clearly identified

Martine Pierre-Louis and Mugette Guenneguez (right) on the balcony of Mugette's apartment in Seattle.

with specific ethnic groups," Martine added. "I felt a part of the city, but I wasn't a New Yorker."

"Once we were in New York we began to realize how much we had put up with in Haiti under Duvalier," Mugette said. "I was so afraid of men in uniform in Haiti, and I remember vividly the first time I saw men in uniform marching in a parade in New York. I wasn't afraid."

Martine went to Fordham University in New York and was the first of her family to move to Seattle. "I came eleven years ago," she said. "I had seen pictures of the Northwest and was attracted by the mountains, lakes, and sea. When I came, it was just going to be for a year. But that turned into two years, and then I started back to school here. After that the family began to follow."

Mugette came three years ago. "I came for a visit, and it was rainy and overcast and I wasn't impressed," she said. "Haitians need sun. The second time I visited, the weather was great and I said 'Wow! No wonder Martine likes it here.' Then our mother came."

Martine is on the staff of Neighborhood House, a Seattle social work agency which assists people in housing projects. Mugette works part time with Catholic Community Services, helping with refugee resettlement. She is a full-time student at Seattle University where she is working on a master's degree in international business."

Martine and Mugette both are U.S. citizens, but Haiti still exerts a strong pull on them. "Most Haitians return home as often as they can for vacations and family visits," Martine said. "I never want to sever my ties completely."

"As Haitians we have to decide whether to carry the banner as African Americans or remain part of a Haitian minority," Mugette said.

And Martine added, "It was not until after college that I broke out of the confines of my Haitian world and began to identify myself as an African American—with a Haitian background."

REYNOLD DELATOUR has led a full and varied life since coming to the United States from Haiti in 1969 when he was seventeen. He went to high school in Brooklyn and to Manhattan Community College. He was a professional musician in both New York and Miami for ten years, playing bass with several musical groups, including Pluto and Company. In Miami he entered Florida International University and earned a bachelor's degree in sociology. For the past several years he has been a supervisor in the refugee resettlement program for Catholic Community Services in Miami.

Reynold Delatour

Mr. Delatour has long been fully integrated into American life, but like so many other Haitian Americans we met, he remembers his former homeland with great warmth. "I love mountains," he told us. "In Haiti, almost every place you go, you will be in mountains. My mother owns land in the countryside. When I go home, I take pictures, breath the fresh air, visit places I didn't have a chance to see when I lived there. For years I hesitated to go home because I was afraid of what I would find. Then I discovered that I had remembered it wrong. It was beautiful."

Jean Michael Pierre with his children

JEAN MICHAEL PIERRE was a teacher of French in Haiti. Now he is doing unskilled manual work at a plumbing supply company in Tucson, Arizona. In the fall of 1994, Pierre, his wife, and their three children were given refugee status by the American embassy in Port-au-Prince because Pierre, an Aristide supporter, was being hunted by army and police thugs. The Pierre family was brought directly by plane to Tucson, bypassing Miami because of the heavy refugee load there.

Haitians attending night school for migrants in Marion, Maryland. Many Haitians study English in special night classes and leave the migrant stream as soon as they can find jobs.

Life is hard and lonely in Tucson. If there are other Haitians in the city, the Pierres haven't met them. In addition to his job, Pierre is studying English five nights a week at Pima Community College. He is also having to learn some Spanish because that is the language of the crew he works with. But when I asked Mr. Pierre if he would rather go back to Haiti if he could or stay in the United States, he did not hesitate in his answer.

"Stay," he said.

Before Paul took their picture, Pierre bathed his sons and dressed them in fresh clothes. Pierre himself put on a suit and tie. The oldest boy, whose name is Brown Jergens, is going to kindergarten, and his father says he is doing well. As they were getting dressed, I heard Brown Jergens singing "Old McDonald Had a Farm."

For Jeffrey Theus, twenty-two, waiting tables at the Tap Tap, a popular Haitian restaurant in Miami Beach, is a way to make money while he continues his education. Jeffrey is presently taking a fifteen-month training program in medical records coding at the Miami-Dade Medical Center.

Like Jeffrey Theus, Weiselande Cesar came to the United States as a child and went to high school in New York. She also waits tables at the Tap Tap restaurant, but in addition is a professional singer and dancer. She rounds out a very full life going to Barry University in Miami where she is studying business, marketing, and theater.

5

HAITIAN ART

A SPECIAL GIFT

TO AMERICA

THERE IS A SAYING in Haiti that "every Haitian is an artist." While the saying is hardly meant to be literally true, the number of seriously practicing painters in Haiti is astonishing. The book *Haitian Arts*, a careful and thorough study, lists nearly seven hundred professional artists whose paintings are sold in galleries in Port-au-Prince and other Haitian cities as well as in galleries in the United States and Europe, especially France.

Toussaint Auguste, an artist who came from Haiti to the United States in 1967 and who is still painting actively, had this to say: "Painting is vast in Haiti. There are people who paint before they go to school. We can't even explain it. It's a part of us."

Most Haitian artists have been self-taught and have painted in the so-called "primitive" or "naive" style. Their subjects have ranged from realistic rendering of life in Haiti to works featuring voodoo ceremonies and symbolism. Christian religious subjects have been and are still popular; many of the Episcopal churches of Haiti are decorated with murals depicting biblical scenes. In more recent times, an increasing number of Haitian artists have received formal training at several institutions such as the Centre D'Art in Port-au-Prince and are painting in all modern styles. Also, young Haitian artists have been taking advantage of scholarship opportunities to study art in the United States, France, and Mexico.

Haiti's remarkable art tradition and energy have never been fully explained. The tradition clearly reaches back to African mysticism and to the legacy of mask and statue carving brought to Haiti by the earliest slaves. Wood and stone sculpture continue as strong Haitian art forms. The energy, the need to express feelings and emotions, is doubtless rooted in the struggles and the sorrow of the country as well as in the beauty and color of the land.

Hundreds of Haitians who have come to the United States have brought their zeal and artistic talent with them or have developed here as artists. The work of Haitian-American artists is featured in dozens of art galleries in New York, Florida, and California as well as in cities in Arizona, Texas, Connecticut, and other states.

Haitian-American artists are increasingly finding the Miami area an attractive place to live, but the single largest Haitian-American artists' colony is probably still in the Queens, New York, community of Jamaica. Over a hundred seriously practicing artists are at work there. Many of them supplement their art income with other employment, but painting is their main passion and commitment. Many of them regularly exhibit their canvases in Jamaica's Active Art Gallery, which devotes almost all of its space to displaying Haitian art.

In Miami, Burton and Christine Chenet, a Haitian-American couple, are busily pursuing quite different yet in some ways quite related careers. Burt (as he is called by his friends) is an artist whose paintings

Christine and Burton Chenet in their Miami apartment.

are receiving ever-increasing attention and admiration in the art world. He has had individual exhibitions of his work at galleries in Los Angeles; Coral Gables, Florida; New Canaan, Connecticut; and Port-au-Prince. His paintings have been shown in numerous selected group shows in New York and other U.S. cities. He was Artist-of-the-Month at the Museé du Pantheon Haitien in Port-au-Prince in 1991.

Christine, who uses her maiden name Audain professionally, has her own landscape design company called Tropicscape. She took her bachelor of science degree in landscape architecture from Louisiana State University, then worked for a Miami landscape design firm before going into business for herself. Most of her assignments have been with homeowners, but she has also done design work for businesses, including a bank in Little Haiti. Burt is vice-president of Tropicscape. With his artistic background, he has valuable ideas to contribute, but he says modestly, "My job is to go out and buy sandwiches."

Burt's mother is American, his father Haitian. They met while she was in Haiti on a vacation. Because of the dictator François Duvalier, Burt's father had to leave Haiti, so Burt was born in New York. Then Burt's father returned to Haiti because his father (Burt's grandfather) had been imprisoned by Duvalier. When Burt was two, he and his mother were able to return to Haiti, and Burt spent the next twelve years of his life in Port-au-Prince. When he was fourteen, Burt went to a boarding school in Connecticut.

"I had my first art class when I was in tenth grade," Burt told us, "and it was as though I had been struck by lightning. I knew from that moment what I wanted to do in life."

After high school, Burt spent two years at Thiel College in Pennsylvania where he learned the basics of art; he then completed his formal art education with a bachelor of fine arts degree at the School of Visual Arts in New York. In 1985 Burt returned to Haiti where he painted and taught drawing and painting for six years at Ecole Nationale des Arts and at the Centre D'Art in Port-au-Prince.

"I learned a lot about myself and about Haiti during that period," Burt said.

When Aristide was forced out as president of Haiti and exiled, Burt quit teaching and returned to the United States.

CHRISTINE'S family also had trouble with François Duvalier; two of her uncles were killed by the dictator's forces, and her mother was in hiding while she was pregnant with Christine. But they survived that ordeal, and Christine spent her childhood years in Port-au-Prince.

Paul and I talked with Burton and Christine in their airy apartment filled with his large canvases. Against one wall on the living room floor was a weathered old pirogue, a Caribbean dugout canoe. On the porch were several bonzai trees. "My babies," Christine called them.

"My grandmother had a rose garden in Port-au-Prince when I was a child," Christine said. "That was my first exposure to plants. I spent a lot of time outside helping her. Later when I developed an interest in art, she suggested that landscape architecture would be something that would allow me to pursue both interests."

Nodding toward Burton, Christine said, "We've known each other a long time. He played with my brother in Port-au-Prince, and I think he had a crush on my sister then. But we remained friends when we grew up, and I always admired his work."

They were not particularly close, however, and Christine was surprised and touched when, two months after she graduated from Louisiana State University, Burton sent her one of his paintings, a blue underwaterscape. That was in 1991. Two years later they were married.

In his paintings Burton works with Haitian themes and symbols, including those of voodoo, and with their bright colors. In a statement about his art, he wrote, "It is, I feel, my responsibility to create an art

Christine holding the painting Burton sent her when she graduated from Louisiana State University.

by which others can penetrate our culture and know how immensely rich our people are, despite the fact that, in statistics, we are listed among the poorest in the world."

SOPHIA LACROIX lives in Miami. She is Haitian, but in this densely Hispanic city, she is frequently assumed to be Cuban. "People are always coming up to me and speaking Spanish," she says with a laugh. In explaining her light skin, she told us that she traced her family roots and discovered a Dutch buccaneer and a great-grandmother who was French.

Sophia was born in Haiti twenty-five years ago. She went to a private school in Port-au-Prince and started art lessons there when she was ten. In 1984 her family immigrated to the United States and settled in Miami, where Sophia went to Norland Senior High School. Her interest in art continued, and she was president of her high school art club.

Her grades in school were excellent, and her parents, unhappy at the thought of her becoming a struggling artist, urged her to give up the idea of a painting career and aim toward medical school. Sophia went to the University of Florida with that in mind and took a bachelor of science degree in nutritional science. After graduation she decided to work for a while before deciding whether to apply for medical school. It was during that period of reflection that she came to the realization that her art was too important to her to give up, and she returned to painting with a passion.

To support herself Sophia works for the Florida Health and Rehabilitation Service processing applications for Medicare and food stamps. She keeps a camera in her desk in case she meets people whose faces interest her. Sophia lives in a tiny house north of Little Haiti, and the walls are covered with her paintings. Some have a Haitian quality; others do not.

Sophia Lacroix

"I would like to paint all day every day," Sophia said. "Now I cram forty hours of work at the office into four days so that I have long weekends. I come home at five-thirty and then paint from six to ten."

It was while she was in college that she began meeting other Haitians and recaptured the old life that she had begun to forget. "Haiti has such a rich culture with its mixture of African and European art and music and dance," Sophia said. She wants to capture that richness in her paintings.

Sophia's paintings have begun to sell, both at individual showings and to a number of clients who buy her work regularly. She is particularly pleased that she was invited to exhibit her paintings at the National Black Arts Festival in Atlanta during the summer of 1996.

A SLENDER, elegant woman, Elyzabeth Narrow Martineau lives in the Washington, D.C., suburb of Bethesda, Maryland, in a spacious house built by the famous architect Frank Lloyd Wright. She has turned the house into a virtual gallery of Haitian art. A prolific artist herself, many of the paintings on the walls are her own work, but others are by well-known Haitian and Haitian-American artists.

Elyzabeth sells her paintings through a New York gallery. "I love art," she said. "I sell my paintings so that I can buy the paintings of others. While I was growing up, people gave me paintings instead of dolls. I've had an art collection since I was thirteen."

She loves to talk about Haiti. "There are so many Haitis in Haiti. It is a land of surprises. Despite our political problems and our poverty, we have such class. We love art. We all speak several languages, and wherever we go, we make friends."

Elyzabeth does not share the commonly held view that Haiti has a racial or skin color problem. "We never really talk about color in Haiti," she said. "How could we? In my own family, for example, my father was jet black and my mother is blonder than you are. I grew up

Elyzabeth Narrow Martineau

not even realizing that my best friend was darker than I or that I was a shade lighter than she. When I went to get my driver's license here, I didn't know how to describe myself—not black, not white. Finally, I marked the 'other' box. I am café au lait.

"My father was a well-known poet. I never had the chance to know him because he was killed in a car accident when my mother was six months pregnant with me. You know, in Haiti it is women who are in command. They are the doers. When my mother became a widow, she went to Jamaica to learn how to sew. When she returned to Haiti, she became a couturiere and designed and made dresses for well-to-do women. In time, she had a staff of sixteen."

When Elyzabeth was four, her mother remarried. Her stepfather was a very distinguished man, a banker and politician. "It was such a good life," Elyzabeth said, remembering her childhood. "We were so free! We had the beach and the mountains. There was nothing to fear. We trusted everyone." Recalling those days and looking at her paintings, she added, "You never forget the colors of your country. They are like a perfume."

But those days of freedom and wonder were to end too soon. In 1957 the tyrant François Duvalier came to power in Haiti, and Elyzabeth's stepfather was caught almost immediately in the dictator's web of evil. Three of her stepfather's friends and professional associates were killed by Duvalier's assassins; her stepfather was thrown into prison and kept there for four years.

Her mother was also imprisoned for several months. When she was released, she and Elyzabeth took refuge in the Argentinian Embassy. They applied for entrance to the United States, and their application was approved. They went to Washington, D.C., where two of Elyzabeth's uncles had settled.

Elyzabeth's mother opened a couturiere establishment in the upscale Georgetown section of Washington. She made clothes for the

70

Her backyard is Elyzabeth's favorite place to work.

rich and famous and sold fashionable accessories; her client list included the Kennedy women and the wife of the Secretary of State. "Her French helped," Elyzabeth said, with a smile. "Washington was a very snobbish city then.

"I hated school in Washington," Elyzabeth said. "It's very hard when you don't speak the language. So I went to a girls' school in France. After that I studied in Switzerland. When I came back to the United States, I went to Stanford University and studied textile design. Then I went to the Corcoran School of Art in Washington."

Elyzabeth was married for seven years, divorced, and returned to Haiti. She ran an art gallery there and married a military man, who died while she was pregnant—the same thing that happened to her mother. Her present husband is a corporate lawyer, an American. "The only spices my husband knew before I entered his life were salt and pepper," she said, laughing. "You can imagine what we have in Haiti and what he eats now."

Elyzabeth has four children by her three husbands.

Whenever possible, Elyzabeth paints in her backyard, but she also works in a small room in her basement, which is full of canvases. "I work late at night when there are no telephones ringing, no interruptions," she said. "I have to balance all my roles—wife, mother, artist. It isn't easy."

6

TO BE HAITIAN AMERICAN

▼

THROUGHOUT our talks with Haitian Americans, Paul and I were struck by how many of them felt compelled to keep the Haitian heritage alive in their children even as the children learn to be Americans; how they felt that Haitian Americans have a responsibility to help each other; how they believed it is important to help other Americans learn more about Haitian Americans and Haiti. We found some or all of these beliefs in Haitian Americans such as Michel Dodard, Vladimir Lescouflair, Jan Mapou, Larry Pierre, Lesly Prudent, and Yolande Thomas, to name only a few. In Jean and Jessie Colin we found perhaps the ultimate expression of what many feel it means to be Haitian American.

"WE WERE living the American dream."

Paul and I were talking with Jean and Jessie Colin and their three sons in their comfortable home in Cooper City, Florida. Jean, however, was not talking about their life in Florida but rather about his and his wife Jessie's years in New York after leaving Haiti.

Jessie left Port-au-Prince in 1965, at the age of thirteen, joining her mother who had immigrated to New York ten years earlier. Jessie stayed with a great aunt in Haiti until her mother could support her in New York.

Jean finished high school in Haiti; in 1971, when he was twenty, he came to New York to go to college. He lived with his brother who was already there. "Haitians believe in education," Jean said. "We came because we wanted to improve our lives, not because we were refugees. All Haitians aren't political refugees." And he added, "When we first come, we are amazed by all of the scholarship opportunities that exist."

Jessie went to Francis Scott Key High School in Brooklyn, then to Hunter College in Manhattan where she completed a bachelor of science degree in nursing in 1974. Later she took a master's degree from Hunter in nursing education and nursing administration. Jean earned a bachelor's degree in business administration from Bernard M. Baruch College, one of the colleges that, like Hunter, comprise the City University of New York.

In Haiti Jean and Jessie had been childhood friends, living in the same neighborhood. In New York they renewed their friendship, and in 1976 they were married. After graduation from college Jean went to work for the Chemical Bank of New York, then Allstate Insurance, then Mutual of America, improving his position with each move. Jessie became a team leader and staff development instructor at the Cabrini Medical Center in New York City. Later she was associate director and then director of the New York State Nurses Association.

The Colin family in their Cooper City home. Left to right: Frantz, Pierre, Jessie, Jean, and Paul, standing behind his father.

Jean and Jessie bought a home in Commack, a small upper middle class city on Long Island, within easy commuting of their work in New York City. Their three sons, Frantz, Paul, and Pierre, were born there. Within a few years after leaving Haiti, the Colins had good educations, good jobs, a house of their own, and a wonderful family to go in it.

They were indeed living the American dream.

But slowly Jean and Jessie began to see a flaw in that dream, a flaw that became more and more apparent as the years went by. "On Long

Island we were isolated in an all-white community," Jean explained to us. "The boys went to good schools and did well. They had school friends and neighborhood friends. But there were no Haitian-American kids or African-American kids for them to be with. They couldn't help having certain problems of self-confidence, a certain questioning of their identity.

"The boys did speak Creole and still do, fluently," Jean added. "Our housekeeper in Commack was Haitian and spoke nothing but Creole, and that helped them with their Creole."

"We have a strong sense of family," Jessie said. "We have taken the boys to Haiti several times to see their grandparents, uncles, and cousins. They could speak Creole to their grandparents. That was wonderful. They could go down to the corner store and buy candy just like the other kids."

The language and the visits to Haiti helped, but they weren't the same thing as being in a place where there were other Haitian Americans. The family could have moved to another community in New York where they would have been surrounded by Haitian Americans and Haitian culture. But Jean and Jessie were beginning to have other thoughts: thoughts about Florida. They had friends there. Jean's younger brother Phillip and his family had moved there. The quickly growing Haitian population in Florida was in a period of rapid development and change, just as the Haitian community in New York had been in the sixties. There would be a chance to do new and important things in Florida.

"And there was the climate," Jean said. He did not say more, nor did he need to. The difference between New York and Florida weather has been a factor in the move south of many Haitian Americans.

Jean and Jessie Colin sold their house in Commack and moved their family to Florida in 1989. The decision was made more difficult by the fact that they both had good jobs in New York. As director of the

Frantz earns spending money by working several hours a week at the Pembroke Pines Racquet Club. He makes reservations for court time and sells equipment.

New York State Nurses Association, Jessie had a particularly senior position. At that time the association had thirty thousand members; Jessie directed a staff of forty-five, both professional and administrative, and managed the association budget of well over a million dollars. Finally Jessie took a step that made their move to Florida a certainty: she resigned as director of the nurses association!

To make the move financially possible, Jessie accepted a two-year appointment as Visiting Assistant Professor of Nursing at Florida Atlantic University, and Jean made arrangements to do some work for an insurance company in Miami. They bought a home in Cooper City, a small, civic-minded municipality of twenty thousand in Broward County, about an hour's drive from Miami's Little Haiti. Their house is in a pleasant neighborhood and only a few doors from the house of Jean's brother Phillip, who manages a nearby fast-food restaurant. One of Jessie's former classmates also lives in the neighborhood.

The move has been all that Jean and Jessie hoped it would be for their sons. Frantz, seventeen, and Paul, fourteen, go to Cooper City High School. "They have a good support group there," Jean said. "There are at least ten other Haitian-American students plus African Americans and other ethnic groups. It isn't at all like Commack." Pierre, eleven, goes to Pioneer Middle School and has a good mix of friends.

Frantz, now a senior, has had an outstanding high school career. He has consistently been on the principal's honor roll. He is a member of both the high school swimming and water polo teams and was captain of the swimming team in 1993. In October 1994 he received the joint Cooper City High School-Cooper City Citizen of the Month Award. In addition to his school achievements, the award cited Frantz for his community services: delivering meals to the homeless and wrapping and delivering gifts for abused children. Frantz will be a pre-medical student at Barry University in Miami next year.

Perhaps influenced by his father, Paul Colin is interested in business and accounting and is a member of the Cooper City High School Decca Club, a national organization whose members share an inclination for business and commerce. Paul is a talented soccer player and is a regular on one of the teams in the Cooper City soccer league.

Paul, foreground, in a Cooper City soccer league game.

Pierre, also with an eye to business and making money, earns $25 to $35 a week during the soccer season waving flag as a judge during the games. He attended a special training program to qualify for the job.

Jessie completed her two-year assignment at Florida Atlantic University and accepted an assistant professorship of nursing at Barry University. Since coming to Cooper City she has devoted as much time as possible to community service. She is on the Multi-Ethnic Advisory

Board of Broward County. She was a member of the Haitian-American Chamber of Commerce of Broward County task force, and she took part in a Haitian Nurses Association drive to immunize children in Broward and Dade counties.

Jean has become executive director of the Haitian Health Foundation of south Florida. The foundation, of which Jessie was a founding member, is an organization of Haitian-American doctors and nurses whose mission is to deliver health-care services, provide health education, and give health counseling to Haitians, Haitian Americans, and other ethnic minorities. The programs are all geared to the specific needs of the Haitian population of south Florida and are delivered in a way that is most understandable and acceptable in terms of Haitian cultures. One of the foundation's projects has been the conducting of AIDS awareness workshops in Broward County. Another has been establishing wellness centers in elementary schools.

In addition to his duties as executive director of the Haitian Health Foundation, Jean has created a south Florida radio program designed to give young Haitian Americans more information about their roots and to emphasize the positive qualities of Haitian culture and Haitian-American accomplishments. Through the Haitian Health Foundation he has also created a series of television programs for the purpose of giving viewers a better understanding of the Haitian-American communities of south Florida.

The move from New York to Florida took courage, but, without any doubt, Jean and Jessie Colin and their sons are still living a splendid version of the American dream.

7

A LOOK
AHEAD

▼

THE SITUATION in Haiti is still uncertain and probably will remain so for a long time, but there is room for cautious optimism. As Jean-Bertrand Aristide's four-year term as president came to an end (under the Haitian constitution a president cannot serve two consecutive terms), a new presidential election was held in December, 1994. René Préval, a good friend of Aristide, won the election and was sworn in as Haiti's new president on February 7, 1995. Thus, for the first time in Haiti's history, a peaceful, democratic presidential succession took place. President Préval has pledged himself to carrying on reforms begun by Aristide, including lessening the power and influence of the Haitian army.

Aristide will continue to be a powerful, though unofficial, voice in Haiti's politics and international affairs. He has stressed the importance of economic aid from the World Bank, the International Mone-

A Haitian rests for a moment from his labors in the citrus groves of central Florida. Thousands of Haitian boat people began their quest for survival in the United States as migrant farmworkers in Florida and other East Coast states, and many still continue in that work. Although it is seasonal and requires constant movement, migrant farmwork offers the only chance of employment for many Haitians.

tary Fund, and the United States. He has warned that, unless the government can create jobs, Haitians will try again to leave the country even though there is no political oppression. The government cannot "feed the people with words only," Aristide has said. "We would like to see them with work, jobs, and food, not just words."

By the end of 1995 only about fifteen hundred of the original twenty thousand U.S. troops remained in Haiti. In April, 1996, the last eighty-two American soldiers, who had been attached to a United Nations force, left Haiti. The small U.N. multinational force of nineteen hundred troops, mostly from Canada and Bangladesh, will stay in Haiti as a precaution for maintaining peace and stability. How long the U.N. mission will remain beyond mid-1996 has not been decided.

The American military presence will not disappear completely, however. The Army's "Exercise Fairwinds" calls for rotating small groups of about two hundred military engineers for six-month tours of duty in Haiti. They will help with road repairs, building repairs, including schools, and, as a military spokesman said, "show the flag and be visible."

TOTALLING about half a million, the Haitian minority makes up a small but significant percentage of the U.S. population today. Because the restoration of democracy in Haiti has brought about a sharp decline of boat people, the Haitian rate of growth in the United States is almost certain to decline; but natural increases (surplus of births over deaths) of Haitians in America plus legal immigration will add several thousand to the total each year.

'Haitian immigrants had brought with them the qualities that had been valued in all other immigrant groups: a willingness to work hard to achieve their goals, a deep desire for education, a strong family loyalty and support. A 1990 U.S. Census Bureau study showed that of 140,000 employed Haitian immigrants, 34 percent were working in service jobs; 20 percent were laborers; 21 percent were technical, sales, or administrative workers; 14 percent held managerial or professional positions. Of 70,000 Haitian immigrants enrolled in school, an astonishing 49.2 percent were in college. Of 175,000 Haitian immigrants twenty-five or more years old, 57.6 percent were high school graduates, and 16.1 percent had bachelor's or graduate college degrees. A study of 72,000 Haitian immigrant families showed that 25 percent were buying homes or already owned them. The American dream is more than an empty phrase for these immigrants from a beautiful but troubled island in the Caribbean.

Perhaps the greatest handicap that Haiti has suffered in its unhappy history has been isolation. It is a black nation in the midst of Hispanic and Anglo nations. It is a Creole- and French-speaking nation in a hemisphere of Spanish- and English-speaking nations. Its African cultural heritage, including voodoo, has set it apart from its neighbors. It is possible that the growing number of Haitian Americans will foster an understanding of and communication with Haiti that will be critical to its development as a new century begins.

BIBLIOGRAPHY

Anthony, Suzanne. *Haiti*. New York: Chelsea House Publishers, 1989.

Bloncourt, Gérard. *Haitian Arts*. Paris: Edition Nathan, 1986. (Translation by Elizabeth Bell).

Booth, William. "'Work, Work, Work': In Little Haiti, Life Is Hopeful but Hard." *The Washington Post*, May 19, 1994.

Cheong-Lum, Roseline Ng. *Haiti*. New York: Marshall Cavendish, 1995.

Grenier, Guillermo J. and Alex Stepick, III, ed. *Miami Now! Immigration, Ethnicity, and Social Change*. Miami: University Press of Florida, 1992.

Hanmer, Trudy J. *Haiti*. New York: Franklin Watts, 1988.

Kurlansky, Mark. "On Haitian Soil." *Audubon*, January-February, 1995.

Pierre-Pierre, Garry. "Haitian Artists' Colony Flourishes in Queens." *The New York Times*, April 8, 1995.

Portes, Alejandro and Alex Stepick. *City on the Edge: The Transformation of Miami.* Berkeley: University of California Press, 1993.

Ringle, Ken. "Island Paradox." *The Washington Post*, October 28, 1994.

_____. "Where Reality Loses Its Grip." *The Washington Post*, October 25, 1994.

Sontag, Deborah. "Haitian Migrants Settle In, Looking Back." *The New York Times*, June 3, 1994.

Suro, Roberto. "Haiti's History of Isolation Makes U.S. Crusade Harder." *The Washington Post*, July 25, 1994.

Viglucci, Andres. "Haitian Play an Ode to Price of Freedom." *The Miami Herald*, November 20, 1994.

INDEX